ler

Sasho Dimoski

ALMA MAHLER

Translated from the Macedonian by Paul Filev

DALKEY ARCHIVE PRESS

Originally published in Macedonian by Kultura as *Alma Mahler* in 2014.

Copyright © 2014 by Sasho Dimoski
Translation copyright © 2018 by Paul Filev
First Dalkey Archive edition, 2018.

Library of Congress Cataloging-in-Publication Data
Names: Dimoski, Saéso, author. | Filev, Paul, translator.
Title: Alma Mahler / by Sasho Dimoski ; translated by Paul Filev.Other
titles: Alma Maler. English
Description: First Dalkey Archive edition. | Victoria, TX : Dalkey Archive,
2018. | "Originally published in Serbian by Kultura as Alma Maler in 2014"
-- Verso title page.
Identifiers: LCCN 2017036701 | ISBN 9781628972368 (pbk. : alk. paper)
Subjects: LCSH: Mahler, Alma, 1879-1964--Fiction. | Mahler, Gustav,
1860-1911--Fiction. | Musicians' spouses--Fiction. | Married women--Fic-
tion. | Vienna (Austria)--Fiction. | Psychological fiction. | GSAFD: Bi-
ographical fiction.
Classification: LCC PG1196.14.I416 A4613 2018 | DDC 891.8/193--dc23
LC record available at https://lccn.loc.gov/2017036701

www.dalkeyarchive.com
Victoria, TX / McLean, IL / Dublin

Co-funded by the Creative Europe Programme
of the European Union

Dalkey Archive Press publications are, in part, made possible through the
support of the University of Houston-Victoria and its programs in creative
writing, publishing, and translation.

CONTENTS

Alma Mahler

PIANO.

PIANO.

DEATH

Who am I?

Where is this day headed and where will it lead me? What's to become of me over the course of this day?

It's of no consequence now.

Paris is at one end of the world. My world is at the other end. If it were in my power, Paris would not exist. Nor the other end of the world. I would have time to climb aboard a different train, toss my suitcases onto another platform. Toss them, and even thoroughly wreck them. I could, if I wanted to. It makes no difference whether Paris or I exist. Or any other city. For a long time it was just you who was important. I was your shadow. Alma Mahler, the failed composer. Alma Mahler. Your devoted shadow. Your wife, lover, the mother of your dead child, your governess, cook, nurse. Both your feeling of dread and your sense of security. I, Alma Mahler. With countless broken smiles, with dull eyes, and various masks. A mask for every feeling. For every habitual folly.

Why have you aged, Alma? Why are you ugly? Why are you pale? Why do you get scared? Where is your face, Alma? Where are your eyes? Where have all your years gone, Alma? Where has your time gone?

It's immaterial now. Vienna is at the other end of the world. My world is here. You're here. The railway station. A few suitcases. One for every new feeling. For every loss. You're here. I'm coming with you so that you can die. You said: "You and I will live forever." You said that you conduct in order to live, that you live in order to compose. You said that the only spark in your music is my existence. Symphony No. 6. All are dead. A symphony of death. You said that my soul is the grandeur of the opening of the second movement. That it is life. I smiled. That's why I'm here now. In fact, everything has been about you from the start. I was a misfortune to myself, but a lucky circumstance for you. Things depend on each other. So do people. If not for you, I would never have been the person I am. But, had I not existed, you would always be Gustav Mahler. Another Alma Mahler would have been found. Some other person.

Do you remember the summer of 1901?

It was hellishly hot. An inferno. Symphony No. 6. The death of your brother Otto. There were many tears, Gustav. And much music. I thought I would go crazy. I thought you were losing your mind. That I was losing you. I was afraid. A summer of fear. Then—the symphony was finished. I was engulfed by the saddest music in the world. It rang in my ears like fear. It lay in wait for me like a beast. You released it from inside you. If not, it would surely have spelled your end. Relief, Gustav.

The world appears better from this railway station. I resolved to love you, that there would be no other love for you like mine. You drew your inspiration for creating music from me. But I'm not doing it out of pity or a sense of obligation. I'm doing it because I want to. To be here. For you to tell me that our love will last forever, until the universe ceases to exist.

Two more weeks to live. You know it. I sense it. In love, one always knows when those we hold dear will cease to exist. One prepares for it. In fact, one prepares for loss one's whole life. One fears it. Perhaps that's why love sometimes fades, and then shines forth again. At most, another two weeks. After that, empty seats.

Where to after that, Alma Mahler?

Nowhere, for the next fifty years. Or more. Or less. Nowhere. After that comes darkness. Perhaps something will happen in the darkness. Or nothing will happen. I can't possibly know. I can't imagine anything. This railway platform and this tiny compartment weigh heavily on my mind. I'm starting to get a sense of their apparent void. Women are cursed by feelings of foreboding, the way that men are condemned to blissful ignorance. Each of us has a talent, Gustav. I'm fortunate to possess yours, which in turn develops my talent for survival. One day I will admit that I chose to be an unhappy woman in happy circumstances. It's difficult to devote yourself to a man who lives for something that exists only inside his head, and that needs to be understood by the whole world. Considerable difficulty. Prodigious talent.

Sometimes I wonder to myself: what would have become of us if you weren't who you are? Would I have been equally happy in unhappiness? Would I have chosen lovers over love? I left Max at the last railway station. One doesn't exist on a simple desire to live. Motives are called for. They're essential. My motive has always been the same: silencing the noise that disturbed your work. I was your barricade against the outside world. Against artificial sounds. I imbued your music with the sounds of nature. You were my barricade against the world— because I was always simply satisfied with the events in your life. Your actions, the gleam in your eyes, our story within them. My happiness in them. Our whole world in a single glance between the flicker of lashes. The two of us there, Gustav. One glance is all it takes for a life to be lived between skin and bones, to fill you with delight, to be all around you, to be your hidden strength that raises your spirits when the day is bad, when there is no kind voice. When there is no good time.

We had time, Gustav. Time stood still when we weren't in it. It came to a halt, and nothing took place here or elsewhere. Nothing. We always had time. Always. Every wrong righted in the present, and smoothed over for the future. Every unspoken word for every innermost place within the soul, for every rise and fall within it. Every you for every I, for the various forms the days took, and that slumbered at night. And when we awakened our time, you and I always knew that on the other side of the looking glass stands the unknown. Something only we two could know. That we still know. And that we live today, in these final days that I drag along with me like shackles.

"Alma?" you murmured, lifting your heavy gaze toward me. I merely nodded.

"The birds, Alma. Look at them."

A flock of black birds was flying over our heads. Black birds that looked like a cloud, behind which the most terrifying secret was hidden. In the flap of their wings I saw my own flight. I wanted to have my own flock. But I was alone, like the bird that remains behind beneath the eaves so that all the others can have a place to return to when they get weary of the heavens.

"They're leaving," I said.

"They're leaving, Alma. We're leaving too," you whispered, and smiled.

We were leaving. Fleeing ourselves. We were heading to new horizons, to unexplored regions that froze the blood in my veins. Landscapes, places, and people of whom I was afraid, Gustav. Of whom I'm still afraid. One shouldn't remain alone with fear. It can devour you. It can devour me, and leave nothing behind.

I've been assailed by a multitude of fears from all the unpleasant situations I have found myself in. I looked those fears squarely in the eye. I observed them, and sympathized with them. They wrapped themseleves around me and fed off me, they mocked me, they kept silent. They cried out, Gustav. They were both powerful and weak. I was strong and weak. Helpless, in despair, absent, happy, and forgotten. I forgot myself. I forgot myself like a deer among a hungry pack. Like a lone deer, Gustav, because there were times when you failed to remember that not a day goes by in which you can forget love. There is no such day, Gustav. That's what gives rise to disapproving glances and animosity. That's how others make their appearance. We alone allowed them to enter our lives, to come in and to leave.

Love never demanded that of us. Love sought us out. It is still seeking us out. We simply forgot to nurture it, to cultivate it. To be with it when we were without ourselves. We forgot, Gustav. And when a person forgets love, it forgets him.

"Where are we going?" I asked.

"Where we must get to, Alma," you whispered, turning your head away.

We made it to many places, Gustav. We hurried, we took our time, but in the end we got there. We went everywhere we were meant to go. Everywhere. We had the whole world before us in our eyes and it still remains there. In our eyes, in our silences, in our weariness. I'm tired, Gustav. I'm so tired that, sometimes, I don't have the strength to let the day happen to me. And in that moment, I think about how little time there is left. That keeps me awake. Because of that, I don't sleep at all. I create memories that I will carry with me everywhere I go. All of these images—this compartment, you in your seat, the shifting scenes of day into night through the window, the paltry meals, the smell of tea, the crumpled newspapers purchased at random out of some strange habit, the creased edges of this dress, the white gloves that have yellowed—all of these images at which I stare silently will be mine, just mine. That's all that time has seen fit to leave me, besides all the scars and marks carved upon my body and in my soul.

Soon you will be gone. But, you will remain here forever, somewhere. In some corner, in a musical note. Not just in one. In every note. In every sound. In every desire. Love can't die, Gustav. Neither can music. It will endure. It will flourish. It will have you always. That's how this world remembers, and how the heavens remember, exactly like those birds that never forget their way home. That's how you will appear: as good tidings for future generations, as a pair of eyes lit up with a flash of inspiration, as a smile on a face. That's how they will remember you. And me, Gustav? I will live in your memory throughout time. I will rescue from oblivion all of those little things that are known only to us. I will archive your soul, maintain it. As if it were the most precious thing that life has brought me. With a lover's faithfulness, with a mother's sacrifice. With all that remains of you for me, that remains just mine, Gustav. Just mine. Just ours.

Symphony No. 1

TITAN

Gustav? Gustav? Gustav!? Gustav! Gustav!!

You can have any name you wish, Gustav. You might even be called a fabrication. I sometimes used to think that you were a figment of my imagination, a product of my deepest fantasy. It seemed to me as if your talent were merely an imaginary form of what I myself wished to possess and never had. That it was a reason for love. How stupid you are, Alma! Stu-pid! You needn't be just a shadow. You can be an eminently proud shadow. Pride and stupidity. Stupidity and pride. A simple list of priorities. I'm suffering from a seemingly unending loquacity. My head is pounding. Sometimes I have nothing to say, yet my head still pounds. You ought to keep silent, Alma! You must! Stupid and silent Alma Mahler. There should be a sign on my back that reads: Stupid and silent Alma Mahler, unable to die for the sake of herself, instead she died a little for others.

Alma wouldn't permit herself that small death that was hers only. She wouldn't allow herself that freedom. That's why she ended up the way she is: an unhappy consequence of time that never ceases to run, time that long ago stopped being her ally. Alma Mahler who gave up!

I gave up, Gustav. I gave up long ago. Now I simply exist from day to day. I haven't felt alive in a very long time. Nothing pleases me. Nothing saddens me. Nothing and no one can make me happy. As time passes, people go by with it. Nothing remains after people have departed, Gustav. Nothing but other people who spend their days remembering others, kept alive merely by staring at the photographs of smiling faces taken in happier times. I'm one of those people. Today I think the reason for my continued existence is precisely my memories.

No, Gustav. The reason that I'm alive today is for the sake of others. For my loved ones. For you, Gustav.

Someone's laughing. Perhaps it's me who's laughing. Perhaps I hear myself. Oh, if only I could hear myself laugh again! I used to know how to laugh. While you shut yourself up in your little boathouse by the lake, I would laugh and run all around. I felt as if the whole of Austria was at my feet. No, as if the whole world were at my feet! In fact, I couldn't have cared less about who was ruling the world because all things began and ended with your music. You had begun to be heard. To resound. I could hear you. I became Alma Mahler with a capital "M" and a small "a."

Some people are destined to live for others. As if they've been given a mission. Sacrificing their own interests by constantly putting others before themselves. I always knew that it would be like that, Gustav. I was here so that you could be someone important. Someone significant, Gustav. Without making demands, without asking for anything. Simply to be here. So that nature could be near you and within you. There are some things I've never understood. Probably because they're not meant to be understood. I only made sense of them as readymade facts. Not everything is knowable. If everything were knowable, wonder and enchantment would cease to exist and we would become rather ordinary.

I could be quite ordinary. Perfectly ordinary. Just plain Alma. The wife of a butcher. Working in her husband's shop, slaughtering pigs. Drenched in blood my whole life. There would be no difference. The blood of your work is on my hands. Your rage, your emotional weakness, your curses, accursed notes. It would be better if the music were to remain inside the composer's head. In your case there would be far less suffering. But the world would be nothing without art. And I wouldn't be Alma Mahler.

I remember when I saw you for the first time. I fell in love with your funny nose and your glasses—through the lenses, I saw my own face in your eyes and recognized something. I'm not sure exactly what it was that I recognized. I've always shunned explanations. I knew that's what you are. What you should be in order for me to be yours. Yours . . . Yours? I was never yours! There wasn't anything that was just mine. Even my lovers belonged to you. All of my days were yours. And still are. I can't escape that. With the passing of the years I succeeded in making something useful out of all that, or at least I convinced myself that I had. What happened to us? Did my judgement lead me astray? Did I end up being mistaken, Gustav? Mistaken, stupid, former Alma Mahler? A different me, someone who never liked herself?

Nothing can be the same when a person ends up alone. I was alone. And I am alone. After us, I was left to bear the burden of my own loneliness and solitude. I met many people, none of whom could fill my emptiness, the gaping hole in my heart. And that's why I gathered up your scores in my arms. I gathered them up and danced with them. I danced to all your music. With you, with the scores, with their notes. I danced with my forlorn and lonely time. I didn't want anyone to see me. I didn't want to see anyone. But I had to, Gustav! I had to go on after us. To live, and go on with life. After us, the greatest burden fell to me. And all of that baggage, this baggage, some other baggage, mine or someone else's. And all the truths within them. Truths that would emerge after us. After you. Truths that weighed on me and at the same time affirmed that, one day, one will have to bear one's burden alone. Entirely alone. Without anyone's help. The one mission left would be to recollect that there had once been someone with whom one had shared the burdens. The knowledge that I had you, even when I thought that everything was lost. Today, I know what is lost: my opportunity to have done something worthwhile with my life. Still we've left behind many good things. Many things of lasting value, Gustav.

I remember when you began to write *Titan*. Symphony No. 1. You took the form of the person you wanted to be. Foresight or madness? I thought it was madness. You knew that it was foresight. Especially with regard to the arrangement, with its weight. Something revolutionary was taking place, something I couldn't understand. You explained it to me. I thought I was stupid. That I was totally stupid. Then I thought that you were mad, that all of that could only exist in your head. Alma Mahler was for the first time approaching the stars. I felt like Adam in that fresco who, despite all his efforts, can't quite reach God's outstretched hand.

It was then that you said to me:

"Beethoven wrote the greatest number of symphonies. Nine. I will write more. And you and I will love one another, Alma. Forever."

Love each other forever? Do you know where that "forever" is today, Gustav? Do you know where my forever has gone? It has withdrawn somewhere far away and I can no longer see it. My eyes have grown old with age. They are clouded. You might even say unseeing. I no longer see things the way I used to. But, however far away they are, however poor my sight may be, I can still discern their presence. In my forever, there is an old woman who desperately waits. An old woman whom time has forgotten, who sits on this chair, in this totally insignificant apartment, in one of the world's countless cities. The old woman that I've become, and who gets scared. Who is terribly afraid that she has no one to squeeze her hand. That's where my forever is, Gustav. In the clasp of this old and spotted hand that is empty.

I was threatened by your transformation. I was scared of what would become of me after you had changed. Changes were taking place daily. There was no end to them. In fact, I don't remember how they even began. You were staring at your reflection in the quiet stillness of the lake, and discovered there a kind of music. You said to me:

"Listen, Alma. Listen!"

I was unsure what it was I was meant to hear. It was silence. Total silence, occasionally broken by my rapid breathing.

If only you knew how much I cried, Gustav. I ran off from your little boathouse and sobbed. I saw you taking a swim in the lake. That's when I returned. You lifted me in your arms, all wet, and said to me:

"Don't be frightened, Alma. It's just music!"

Then you smiled. You smiled at me with all of your music. Contained in that smile was the spark of life passed to man. My man. To whom I gave the best part of myself.

At that time you still knew how to smile, at least with your eyes. That's how I smiled at you also. I smiled with my whole being, simply because all of the things in my life grew better and more important alongside you. They prospered within us. We were a kind of soil in which every seed bore a lavish crop. We fed off each other. We were happy, weren't we, Gustav? When one experiences a sense of mediocrity, is it then that others begin to make an appearance in one's life? I don't know. What I do know is that sometimes we would look away and swallow our tears. We swallowed our tears and opened our arms as a way for us to warm our hearts, at least for a moment. It was a different kind of heat. One that seared us, instead of warming us. We wounded one another. We violated our love and it beat a hasty retreat. But it didn't escape entirely. It came back. We succeeded in our fight for it not to forget us. That's why I'm here today. That's why this railway platform is here.

Life never throws us burdens greater than we are able to bear. And we bore them: joys, sorrows, ordeals. We gazed at the sky and saw our burdens within it. The sky—distant and blue, our burdens—always new and different. The sky gray, our burdens scattered all around. We looked at each other and knew that we had strength. Strength, Gustav. That's what keeps me alive. The strength that time has given me, and because of which there is no burden I cannot bear to the end of the road. This path, this train, and this platform today are sapping all my strength. At the same time they're making me stronger. When one's strength is gone one realizes the importance of perseverance. It's quite necessary, Gustav. One must stand firm if one is to remain true to oneself to the end. To the end of it all, to the final breath. That's why I smile. And laugh. Because I know that my end has occurred on this road a long time ago and that I will remain behind in every place. I will remain inside us, Gustav.

Symphony No. 2

RESURRECTION

ONE SHOULD ALWAYS REMEMBER to laugh. How easy it is to forget. But one can learn to laugh again. Everything can be learned, Alma. Besides talent. Either you have it or you don't. As for you, Alma, you were spectacularly untalented at everything. You always did have an impeccable talent for suffering, and for love—if by love what is actually meant is a pathological attitude toward the self for the better part of one's existence. At times I felt a strange urge to rip off my skin and set it aflame. To examine my own naked existence: it's possible that the muscles on my face alone learned to remain in a twisted grimace; that my blood took on the color of the ink with which you wrote your notes; that my muscles had withered to the point that they were no longer able to work on their own, and instead required an external stimulus—some sort of magic charm: your voice, your eyes, your simple needs. Alma Mahler, an automaton ministering to the needs of the great Gustav Mahler. That was enough for me. More than enough, because I had the greatest gift one can hope to receive: the chance to love. Life is brief, Gustav. So fleeting that, at times, it appears like a pleasant dream from which you emerge with the hope that at long last you will begin to live, only to discover that everything has ended. All stories come to an end, one way or another. No story remains open-ended. That's why people tell stories: so that their hopes and dreams, joys and sorrows may be preserved for future generations. Life is nothing if you don't leave behind your story in the best way possible.

At times it comes at great personal cost to have the world at your feet. For the world to exist, Gustav. If I no longer enjoy being blond—I will become a brunette. And though it wouldn't suit my pale complexion, I will wear bold red lipstick. If you no longer wish to be a Jew—you can dress in phony garb and become a Catholic. It would suit your character and position. It would suit your notes. In turn, the notes will sound better together. And the sounds will reverberate all around, enduring beyond all that is yet to come. A superhuman form is being brought into being. You can change as much as you want, Gustav. To be sure, you can and will change throughout your life, but your essence will remain the same. Some people have a clear purpose in life: concern for the spiritual well-being of humanity, while others are concerned for those who are taken up with the problems of the world. In both cases, things come down to the fundamental principle of regard for human life, but one can't be concerned for oneself or the world until one learns to take care of oneself. Ironic, but true. It didn't trouble me being married to a man who was popular with all the opera divas, nor that he devoted his whole life to values determined by the ear. I knew that in my heart. I knew that you would be here after all the fanfare was over. When the circus ended. It wasn't a circus. It wasn't theater. Just plain and simple life. Ordeals, bad days, good days, days that never were, days I wished had never existed, a few incidents worth forgetting, several others etched deep in my memory. That's what remains for me today. All of the things that have ceased to exist. Just that. And very few other things: a chance or intended letter, a stray or planned encounter.

It's easiest to forget here on this railway platform. Things begin on platforms: journeys, encounters, all manner of things—a simple conversation that can change your life. Today, you told me that I had to make a choice from what remains: to decide whether I will go on out of love, the pang of conscience, or a sense of obligation.

There was nothing to choose, Gustav. On this railway

platform, I'm forgetting all the wrongs we committed. I've forgotten that Max ever existed and that all of your whores had ever been born. We will descend from this railway platform together. The journey will continue. You and I must go on. There are so many subsequent stations in life we must reach, so many trains that will take us everywhere that we want to go. I refuse to let our story end like this. I believe in a happy ending for us. I have to believe it, Gustav. That's what keeps me alive. My faith and my dreams—within them lies my strength, simply because once, long ago, I decided that my life would not be a waste of time, but instead it would be a fulfillment in time. That's what meaning is for, Gustav. That's why some people mean more than others do: because they had the inner strength to devote themselves entirely to their dream.

Two more weeks. That's all. After which there will remain silence that will slowly dissolve into your music. Symphony No. 10 is still unfinished. I remember that Max poked fun at you:

"Where is Symphony No. 10, Gustav? How much time do you require to write it?"

You replied rather coldly that it was here all around us, and that he was sufficiently deaf not to hear the pounding of bells, let alone a whole symphony. I wanted to laugh but it would have been unkind. Perhaps in a strange way I loved Max, or I was just trying to be my old self again, that former Alma—full of life, with sparks in her eyes and a passion for life. Or I was simply filling my time while your music was taking shape. Most probably it was the latter, despite the fact that Max made me feel alive, awakening a part of me that had lain dormant for so long. I stopped being someone's wife and became a woman. But, I wanted to be your wife, Gustav. I wanted you to look at me as if there was no other woman on the face of the earth. But those admiring glances died long ago, in a forgotten past, at the beginning of this romance. All that was left between us was that rather dull, ordinary existence in which one day followed another: the silence at morning coffee, looking through rather than at one another, the "good morning" greeting for a bad day that was to follow. But Max used to look at me. He would fix his gaze on me and drink me in, emptying me and then filling me up again. He filled me to the point of surfeit; he gave me a kind of forgotten strength. Alongside Max, I had the feeling that I could relive several youthful lives over again.

One must have a clear idea of one's ambitions. You cannot be everywhere and all things to all people. You can be one thing only. And be a colossus at whatever you choose to do. You must have talent. Either you have it or you don't. Most of the people I knew were gifted and they knew how to use their talent to create universal truths, to create a language with which the whole world spoke, and in that way are certain to be remembered. People are remembered for the truths they leave behind. And we two shall leave behind a truth, Gustav. A great truth wherein the music will replenish all of the blank stares, disclose all that is unsaid, and act as a heartbeat where there is none. Such will be the ripples left behind by us: vanished memories, within the layers of soil, among all of the people who will depart this planet.

Oh, my beloved . . .

I've been hampered by all of life's disappointments. Most of my own experiences have been shrouded in darkness. Totally obscured. I was hidden like the sky behind a dark cloud. You had your music, I didn't have you. I took care of your children. I failed entirely at that also. It's strange what one encounters in life. A simple story can change your day, a day your whole life. And I changed. You saw all that and reveled in your own immutability, at the same time changing the whole world. What did you and I change, Gustav? Was it just ourselves, while everything else stayed the same? Did we stay the same, Gustav? That is the fear that looms large over us all: to have remained the same, for so little to have happened in one's life and with the people in it that we ended up the same. My looks today, these wrinkled hands and this weathered appearance, have made me both sad and full of life. A sadness that cannot be contained, and that spills everywhere. As though I'm spreading contagion. As though I must remain alone so that I don't infect others with myself. There were times when I infected others with myself and held them spellbound. But my enchantment has withdrawn to a place from which there is no return. All that remains is my ability to believe that I still possess some features considered worthy of attention. But no one pays any attention to me besides myself.

This railway platform today is the final change. From now on it's just my face that will age, that will get old until there's nothing left to grow old. The hardest thing is to grow old in this room with all the things that bind the soul to the body. That's why death is an unbearable hardship: one who is in pain draws apart from all of the things that have made one happy in life. Will I die a happy woman, Gustav? Will I be able to say: Alma Mahler was a happy woman? Was I? Am I, Gustav?

I've become a big diary in which are inscribed the lives and desires of all those I have loved, with whom I spent my life. I whiled away time with them, not alone. I didn't have the strength to spend it alone. I always needed someone by my side. That's my greatest weakness, which I attribute to my nature, and the most important battle that I failed to win. To be happy enough alone with myself. My whole life I had a terrible need of others: to share my life with and mean something to someone. I think that everyone has this same need, but mine was like an illness that could only be cured by being with others, when I shared in their existence, in their significance. That's why there were all those men. That's why there were all those supposed lovers. And that's why there was you. Us. And that's why, now, there is this loneliness that at every moment reminds me of all my past achievements. Loneliness that's eating me up from inside, and because of which I neither sleep nor dream. How many dreams did we live out, Gustav? How many times did we look at the sky and count the stars, naming them with all the terms of our endearment? How many times did I see your pupils dilate, your hands shake, reaching for that invisible force from which we both drew our lives?

That's why we will go on forever. And that's why there exists this fear of forgetting. Because of all the stars and dreams within them.

Symphony No. 3

MEMORIES GROW OLD BUT never fade completely. Much like the simple transaction between doctor and patient, whereby treatment becomes a means of prolonging life; also like Pan, who in rousing from his sleep in a forest, ushers in summer all around. But summer is a state of mind, not just the designation of a season. Like all affective relationships, summer's purpose is one of effecting a change in temperament, and mine alters just enough to say that something is different. I don't tolerate change because it's not always for the best. It brings about only short-term pleasures, immediate satisfactions; after that, everything is as if nothing had ever happened. Here and now, change consists of wrinkles around the eyes and broken smiles. You have much about which to keep silent, Alma. You have much to tell. You locked away all of your talents in a small box and buried them ceremoniously. A pointless waste of skills. And of knowledge too, perhaps. You're harmful to yourself, Alma. Kind to others. Gracious tears. Feigning smiles, as your soul cries out. It's better to laugh and cry at the same time. That's the point of broken smiles.

"The birds have flown away, Almschi. They've gone," you whispered.

"They're swifter than us," I replied, and sat down beside you, caressing your cheek.

"Is it possible for any living creature to be swifter than us, Almschi?" you asked.

I stared at your eyes. Your lids fell wearily, and remained closed a long time as the pupils flickered behind them. I said nothing. I didn't know what to say. I just ran my hand gently down your cheek.

"We're even swifter than time, Almschi," you said, and smiled and opened your eyes wide.

"We're on time, Gustav. Right on schedule," I replied quietly, and looked into your eyes. All of the answers to all of the questions were right here, between our glances. Nothing needed to be spoken, Gustav. It was one of those glorious moments, when all one's questions are answered. Everything else had already been said, even in the silences, and in the flight of the flock of black birds behind the white cloud.

The flowers in the meadows have always been a mere reminder: you were a blossom, Alma. After which you became a beacon for meaningless emotions that only meant something to you. No one else saw them, and in that moment when you thought that you were becoming visible, before you in a hazy mirror stood—the sad face of a clown. A tired act. A magic circle of silence. A painful silence. Somewhere deep within me. While all around is noise that threatens to explode inside your head like a watermelon. Somewhere someone may shed a tear for you.

The creatures in the forest have always taught me the same thing: grunts are more appropriate than words. They're rawer. They emerge from deep inside. That's why, you, Alma, are a creature of the forest. A silent forest creature. A nightingale that can't sing. Someone plucked your radiant voice and placed it in the sky above to make certain that it would always shine for them. That it would provide warmth.

People have always said the same thing to me: Alma Mahler, worthy of respect. What's it like living with Gustav Mahler? Does he like coffee? Does he like wine? How long does he sleep? Where does he sleep? What time does he get up? How does he work? What does he like? What doesn't he like?

Alma smiles and replies. She replies with simple answers. She repeats the answers. She organizes Maestro Mahler's formal receptions. She allows her hand to be kissed. She smiles. She knows all the answers to all the questions. She smiles. She smiles. By Jove, how she smiles!

I'm terrified of what the angels tell me. I'm afraid of their words. They say: be careful, Alma. The voices will kill you.

What voices? Are there really voices other than my own? Am I going crazy? Or have I always been crazy? My body can't comprehend the state of my soul. It rebels. It can't accept what's going on inside.

I remember when you told me about the day that Otto died, the same day that you got your job at the Vienna Court Opera. You said that you ran up the stairs with a large bottle of champagne in your hands. So that you could celebrate your success. You discovered Otto on the floor with a gunshot wound to the head. The angels often talk about Otto; sometimes they even say that he was more talented than you. Success is never forgiven, Gustav. Just like failure. Both instances, in one way or another, are fatal in relation to the soul, and they beget a strain around the eyes from either joy or envy.

What love has taught me today is that, like patience, perseverance is always rewarded. Love must sometimes wait for a more propitious time. Now is when our true time begins, Gustav. Without Max. Without those nameless women. Without obligations. Because of desire. It has to be, Gustav. Love owes that to us.

Symphony No. 4

ALMA MAHLER WAS BORN in 1879 under a different surname. That's incorrect. Alma Mahler was born Alma Mahler. Was I in attendance at my own birth, or was it a normal event in which my existence took on a new form?

It was Vienna. No! It was Paris. Vienna existed for only a few moments. There was another Gustav, a Walter, and a Franz as well. Notable personages. Names don't mean a thing. Experiences are what count. There were countless towns. Numerous faces. Various figures, liaisons, incidents. Say what you will, but those few moments in Vienna left their mark.

Wars have also left their mark. Or they will in the time that lies ahead. I fled all those wars. I fled without you and with us. I bundled up your scores, concealing them inside a hidden compartment of my small carrying case. I packed and unpacked them in several new cities. Out of them I built new homes. I fashioned them into sheets between which to dream. They were the bedrock of my assumptions and I was just one Alma Mahler alone.

At this moment I can foresee the future events of my life: you will be gone, life will go off in different directions, with other people, in other homes. The houses and their contents will change. I will change. I will be a different Alma. I will age, but I won't feel myself aging until some future event wipes me off the face of the earth. But Alma Mahler will continue to live on even beyond that. Because of who she is. Owing to all the distinguished names she acquired and is yet to acquire. One must learn to deal with loss. With new habits. I can't stop living just because someone else ceases to exist. Do I exist for myself?

Did I exist for you, Gustav? I existed for many others. On that score, I know that I'll exist for others whom I have yet to meet, who are yet to appear in my life. It's simple. Quite simple. Life just happens and one must allow oneself to become someone.

I feel bad thinking such thoughts now. I feel bad for you too. The loss has not taken place yet, and here I am thinking about how things will unfold. Selfish of me, I know. One makes use of what one has until it's gone. After that one makes use of someone else. Becomes devoted, and in turn earns devotion. A circle. Closed and enchanted. I will never quite understand it. I don't even try to.

Alma Schindler was born on August 31, 1879. Other children may be delivered by storks but Alma was delivered by a raven with a bright yellow beak. She was destined to live a life of extremes: never in the middle, always either in darkness or light. Doomed to a life devoted to boisterous birds that are entirely black. She attracted those kinds of noises, the same way that this railway platform attracts stray travelers.

I knew it would be those kinds of birds that would emerge, even when I met the first Gustav. In the golden hue of his skin I recognized my raven. I laughed to myself. He wasn't laughing. While painting, he generally wore a comical outfit, one that resembled a cloak tied tight around the waist. I remember quite clearly when he painted *The Kiss*. I thought it was my face that had been captured in that fierce, annihilating embrace. Time proved me right. Tight embraces very nearly destroyed me. Then he disappeared, but other notable figures kept on emerging. No ordinary mortals, Gustav. I've always despised common people. There's nothing special about them. No one remembers them and they cease to exist when they stop breathing. I felt pity for them whenever I saw them: smiling faces moving through the streets, with top hats, some wearing monocles, others wearing feathers in lavish hats. I found them amusing. You know, I used to laugh. Those people weren't able to grasp the fact that they wouldn't remain in time, despite being present in it. To be remembered only by somebody who encounters them in a tattered photograph found in an old box completely forgotten in an attic somewhere. With me it has to be different. Perhaps that's why I attract those kinds of men—luminaries, unaware of the world around them and the passage of time, but who will always be a part of both the world and of time. I never had sufficient influence on my own, and that's why I aimed my beauty at those kinds of men. I don't regret it. For any reason at all. Except for the actual losses, but even they occur. Unforeseen—but still they occur. Totally devastating. Leaving lasting effects.

I shut my eyes. Wetness trickles down my cheeks. It carves into my face. I don't want to know how deeply etched the lines are that are left behind. I don't want to know how often floods of tears will burst through my eyes and flow along those crevices, what they will bring, and what they will carry away, how many rivers will flow through the ocean of life. It's just your words and not your stories that repeat themselves to me.

You were telling me that the second movement of Symphony No. 4 is dedicated to death. You experienced the deaths of numerous others, as did I. That's why your music is the way it is: infinite in its structure, revolutionary, cosmic. Death and loss awaken what one has never recognized in oneself before: anger. Unknown fury. Rage when there's no one else to rail against besides, perhaps, oneself. The worst form of rage. About which you cannot do a thing. Ever.

What did you say and what did I keep silent? Only we two know that.

This railway platform here fills me with fury. Total rage. And yet, I smile. I'm smiling like never before. Today you said to me:

"We will love each other, Alma! Forever!"

Symphony No. 5

Adagietto

I COULD BEGIN TO tell you about all the kinds of love that one experiences over the course of a lifetime, but then again, there are no universal concepts of love by which you might understand me. People derive pleasure from things in their own way, above all, because they experience them differently from others. But people don't like each other, Gustav—they *love* each other. Or they don't. That's why I never talk to you about love. I could talk to you about hate, but in life I have despised only those things that are incorporeal: death, absence, emptiness. Emptiness isn't something that can be made manifest. You can place it in a box, turn it into music, but you can never envisage it in its entirety. It cannot be equated with mere absence either, because it's always much more than just that. It's a tremendous feeling of totality. A terrifying totality without end since life is always filled with new kinds of experiences. I could talk to you about those experiences, but something tells me that the time that's left is far too precious to be given over to sad things; besides, I think that I'm quite unversed to talk about such ordeals. What is one able to discuss with a person who is on the brink of death—Happiness? The future? Memories?

"You've specified the wrong things, Alma!"

"What are you referring to, Gustav?"

"What will remain at the end of this huge farce."

"Is this just a farce for you?"

You burst out laughing, roaring hysterically. Fear and panic overcome me. You look deeply into my eyes:

"Don't be frightened, Alma! Fear and happiness are just turns of phrase. Choose the one that causes you the least grief."

Now I'm laughing too. You embrace me. Your hands are shaking. You stare deeply into my eyes:

"All of this was just a stupendous farce, Alma. A huge charade. At times there were too many absent guests. At times those who were part of the fun would slip off quietly, without saying goodbye. Laughter always remains, even when things are difficult. And you want to put things in order while the guests are still here! It doesn't work like that, Alma."

You were always skilled with words, Gustav. And with your silence. For the most part, I took your silence as the absence of any need for conversation, but even so there were many words contained within it. Dark, ominous words. They resound in my head even today. It has always seemed an inherent contradiction to me that a man who creates music expresses his love best in silence. And not just love, but every one of his emotions.

"I'm in no hurry," I replied.

You rise from your seat and stare through the window:

"Do you see all that out there?"

"I see it."

"Well, that's what will change and also stay the same. The stars will look down on us from above as if we're tiny flickers of flame, and they'll never know that a part of them is inside us. You're a star, Alma. I've always known that. While I have only the ability to distinguish stars."

At that moment you fall to the ground. Chest pains. The adagietto from Symphony No. 5 reaches its culmination. I wring my hands. I don't know who to call. I let out a shriek. Someone enters the compartment alone. A man. You begin to come around. A scheduled doctor's appointment at the next stop. I thought—the end is near.

I can't make ready. It's not the same as when you take leave of a living person, when you have to get used to the fact that someone will no longer be in your life. It's difficult, Gustav. Unbearably difficult. I don't know what to say or what to do. I leaf through meaningless fashion magazines and stare at you.

Mostly you sleep. When you aren't sleeping, you say nothing. I can't get the adagietto out of my mind. But the adagietto is hope, happiness, love, fulfillment. I think terrible thoughts: that your demise will set me free and that I'll be able to fall in love with a complete stranger. Unpleasant stories that are to follow this sad story, Gustav. But you're convinced that we will love each other forever.

I cry for myself. You look at me. You think I'm crying for you. I'm crazed with fear, anger, and loathing. Something unbearable is happening within me. I leave the compartment. In the toilet I take off my hat. I let down my hair. I believe that I'm attractive enough to begin a new life somewhere else. A place where I won't feel your absence so acutely. I'm not sure why, Gustav. I'm not sure. I know that it's not right, but I can't do anything about it. I can't do anything about myself. I could get off this train. Not wait for my own unhappy end in your contented demise. There's a curse, Gustav. Something more terrible than a curse. I would call it narcissism. Or even egomania. Have I perhaps forgotten to be concerned about others? It's possible that I exist solely for myself. Alma Mahler and her memories. A delightful relationship. It will endure, Gustav. It will go on forever. With these memories and with the memories that are yet to be made, that will push me closer to the brink. And once there? I will look this Alma Mahler in the eye and I will ask her: was it all worth it?

I can't possibly know. My understanding now is that one only learns as much as time is willing to teach one, and as for me, there's still plenty of time to discover and apprehend things. With what does one fill time that feels like an abyss, Gustav? How much knowledge can you pack in a bottomless pit? All the wisdom of this world? To invent things and feelings anew?

I see emptiness all around.

Virtually everything seems blank.

My hands, my voice. This practically deserted train.

They're empty. Empty, Gustav.

Symphony No. 6

Andante moderato

ALMA? ALMA? WAKE UP, Alma. There's not long to go. In fact, there's precious little time left. And then, Alma? What comes next? Enough with these questions. The passage of time will deliver all that's required. Or it won't. There has to be something more. It doesn't just end here. Not everything. Many things will end.

The twenty-sixth of May, 1906. Four years of wedlock. Only four. Two children. Four years of music, and many more of silence. I learned to keep quiet, Gustav. The echoes of Symphony No. 6 resound for the first time, breaking through my silence, and I understand you. It was meant to be joyous. I was happy. Happy in my own sadness and frustration. Life was going on all around. Bringing with it many good things. I was happy in my sadness. You remained grave and mirthless, smiling only with your sounds. I left you to work. You knew that I wanted to write music. That I wrote music. You said: "Leave music to the composers." I buried my scores on the other side of the lake. I wanted to be a composer. At one point in my life, I probably also wanted to be a painter. I made up for my own lack of talent with the talent belonging to the men I loved. I comforted myself with affection. I thought that I would understand more about how to reach lofty heights. I now realize that one is only as distinguished as one allows oneself to be. Just that and no more. As grand as an orchestra or a piccolo. Like a paintbrush or the entire palette of colors. Sounds and colors beget pain in the same places: in the gaps that remain between them. Music only makes sense if silence exists. Color exists so that light can be distinguished from darkness. A wonderful evening. The twenty-sixth of May. Four years spent being Alma Mahler. What happened to Alma Schindler? Where did her life end? On the nuptial bed? On the piano? On a canvas? I don't know, Gustav. One day she ceased to exist. As you know, one gains one's reputation from others, from those to whom one chooses to commit. It's strange that one often gets lost in others' stories, and becomes someone else. But I've had the strength my whole life to be just plain old Alma. Consequently, I made a decision: plain old Alma would gain a greater reputation if she shared her life with another plain old somebody. Plain old Alma and plain old Gustav. We could have been just that. But then the others came along. I loved Max, you know. Truly loved him. But I loved Alma Mahler much more.

That time in May hasn't existed for years. It ceased to exist the moment the symphony was finished. I believe that it's possible for music to come back, but not to remain. The same goes for people. They come back but they never remain. You were never here, Gustav. And yet, you were always there. I often despised your music. I disapproved of your work. I maintained that it made you sullen. That it was killing you. Many people give birth to great things when they kill something within themselves. You were giving birth to music while becoming dead to me. After that you would stop writing and show me your scores:

"Listen, listen, Alma! That's how much I love you. And how much you hate me."

You knew I hated you. You knew that I couldn't bear all your absences. I came into your life to share it with you, but to a great extent, you were never around. I was all alone. There were the children. If it weren't for them, I would have been dead long ago. There would have been nothing to hold me to this life. I might have abandoned you forever if it weren't for them. When two people love each other their love should resonate all around. But it was only your music that resonated. I wanted you to see me, Gustav! To see me, by Jove! You looked right through me. We weren't sleeping in the same room. I thought that a period of time must elapse before the good times would arrive. No matter how dreadful and appalling it may sound, I think that for me happy moments lie ahead. For every person there exists a kind of happiness. For you it was silence. I learned to love it because I began to detest your music. My face took on a stern expression. I ended up dressing ostentatiously. I wasn't able to tell you what I needed. All I needed was you. But you were nowhere to be found. You know, the days were unpleasant for me also! How unpleasant? As much as yours were pleasing to you. So selfish, Gustav. Self-centered. All you had to do was ask: "How are you, Alma?" You never once asked me that. You assumed that I was well just because my life was comfortable. Because I had your children. Our children. Gustav . . . I can't turn back the clock. Were I able to, I would do the same things over again. I wanted to be there for you, to love you, and for you not to be aware of it. Simply that. Actually, quite early on I discovered that you were positively convinced that I loved you and that I would always be here. I remember when I met Max. He made me feel alive. He awakened everything in me that you had forgotten. Everything I had. And still have. Due to the uneventfulness of my life, I delayed the process of aging. I didn't waste much of what I have. I retained Alma Mahler. No, Alma, that's incorrect. I retained Alma Schindler. Now I know that I never ceased to exist. I merely forgot who I was. But for the right reason. For a good reason, Gustav.

Less than two weeks at best. I think I'm happy. That's why I'm out of breath. I can't breathe. I wrap my arms around myself. I have to be concerned for someone, Gustav! I must! I want to take care of you, do you understand? I have to, Gustav. I beg you, Gustav . . .

Symphony No. 7

NIGHT MUSIC

SEPTEMBER 19, 1908. PRAGUE. The coldest start to autumn I had ever experienced. My body shook all over. Something new stirred within me, or something was being born. I was sitting in the third row. Alma Mahler, wearing an olive-green dress, a hat with netting, a tight-fitting corset, knees trembling, with a rapt expression on my face.

No! A cold twelfth of July! A terribly cold twelfth of July. Maria—dead. Symphony No. 7. Scarlet fever. My spirit broke that day. I shook the bed for hours. For hours, Gustav. Then you entered the room. You put out the candle. You didn't shed a single tear. Not one. I was furious, filled with rage. Dead. Dead beyond any doubt. It takes but a moment for a life to cease to exist. The girl's eyes were open. Her lifeless body warm. You lifted her into your arms. You looked at me, and didn't utter a single word. My life ended with that look. I died on that bed. All subsequent deaths mattered little to me. One of the greatest accomplishments of our love had died. Most of all, it was us who were tormented on account of that death.

You spent the whole summer in the boathouse by the lake. You slept there. You hardly ate. I felt as if I were nursing a dead man. You wouldn't exchange a word with me. Whenever I asked you a simple question, you avoided my gaze. You wouldn't let me in. I peered in at you through the large windows. You were hunched over your scores. Occasionally, you would lift your gaze and stare at the lake. You would take off your glasses and rub your eyes. You massaged your neck deeply with your fingertips. And held a clenched fist tightly against your chest.

"Do you know where I feel pain?" I asked when you emerged from the boathouse one afternoon.

You said nothing. You just stared at me from head to toe. I glared at you.

"Do you know where I feel pain, Gustav!" I cried out.

You stood still. You looked me in the eye.

"Where do you feel pain, Alma?" you asked, your voice barely above a whisper.

I fell to my knees. Like a creature covered in wounds. Like a gaping, festering wound.

You crouched down beside me.

"Where do you feel pain, Alma?" you whispered, taking my head between your hands.

"I feel pain all over, Gustav," and I erupted into tears.

You placed my head on your shoulder. After that, your lips brushed gently against my ear.

"I know, it's painful," you whispered, and you began to weep.

At that moment, I realized there was something to be saved. Amid all our misfortunes, we had something that could be salvaged. Then the thought struck me: that's why I'm Alma Mahler, not just plain Alma. I could never have been just anyone. You must know that I wanted to. I wanted to be completely ordinary. Plain. To not have high expectations. To have happiness catch me unawares, and not worry about achieving anything or becoming anyone important. Some are naturally predisposed toward doing nothing. I'm responsible for everything that's happened to me, and for all that I've done to others. I can't blame anyone else but myself for my current situation. I chose it. It wasn't imposed on me. No one came to me and said: you have to be Alma Mahler. I chose to become that myself. What we do, we do for ourselves. Not for others. With them, never for them.

"Let's go somewhere," I said, grabbing hold of you.

"The Seventh," you replied.

Then I stood up. You remained crouched.

"A whole lifetime hovers over that damned, accursed music!" I cried out.

I ran into the anteroom, picked up a porcelain vase, and smashed it over the piano. You flew into a rage, and grabbed me by the hand.

"What the devil are you doing!" you began to shout.

"Wreaking havoc," I shrieked.

"Stop it, Alma!" you cried.

"You stop!" I shouted back.

You came right up to me and stared into my eyes. Eyes filled with pain and tears. We had the same eyes, you know. The same faraway and empty look in them. You had your music, I just had you.

I had nowhere to go, Gustav, and yet I had all the places in the world. One must flee from one's own misfortune. Mourn what has passed and crave that which must be. I remain here, at least for today. Someone has to save your soul, which I've always known best: one always fills one's life with those one loves. That's why there's no other place for me in this world.

Symphony of a Thousand

Gustav!

Not now! I beg you, Gustav! I beg you!

Strangled breathing. Deathlike pallor. Panic. Fear and panic. One is never quite prepared for it. I thought: so that's it, it ends here, there's nothing further. You smiled gently. A contorted smile. Hope in your eyes.

"Gustav! Gustav!" I called out.

You looked at me, as in those times when your gazes meant something, when you still had them to spare. You stared at me as if seeing me for the first time. A smile. A sincere smile. With that smile, something burst forth within me, Gustav. As if something had been freed. As if you wanted to say to me:

"It was good, Alma. It was good because you were there. And from hereon, it will be better still. This time for you, Alma."

I searched for something to say. A word. You just stared at me. You stared at me with wholehearted approval. I imagined the timbre of your words. I wanted to hear them. For you to tell me that there's no evil done out of love. For you to say something to me, Gustav!

You remained silent, staring at me. I held your face gently in my hands. Someone burst into the compartment. The train came to a halt. End of the line. Brief medical intervention. Raising of arms. Exhaling.

"Imagine the whole universe ringing and echoing. There are no longer any human voices, just planets and stars resounding," you said quietly.

I knew the exact meaning of those words. Symphony of a Thousand. Symphony No. 8. A work of monumental sound.

You were convinced that you'd captured the sounds emitted by the celestial bodies. But that wasn't the case, Gustav. It was only my silence. My unbearable silence within which you endeavored to say something. People have a need for words, to hear that they're loved, that someone cares about them. But there were none.

"Don't wear yourself out," I said to you.

Again, you looked into my eyes and smiled.

I leaned my head down close to your ear.

"For my own well-being, Alma," you said to me.

A teardrop fell from my eye. A single tear. It dripped onto your nose.

"For your own well-being, Gustav. For your own well-being," I said, and kissed your lips.

In that moment, I grasped the significance of what I should have known all along. Some people have love enough for only one thing, others throw their love away. The self-interested have their object of devotion. For some that's a person. You had your music, and whatever else remained need not have existed. That's how unfortunate circumstances arise and how, through no fault of their own, people get caught up in them. I was enthralled by your music. But it developed into an illness. We infected numerous others: you because of your nature, me from love. I don't know what I'm thinking anymore.

You closed your eyes. You were sleeping.

We returned to Vienna. We returned for the final time. Gustav and Alma Mahler. A self-evident death with a life in tow. Difficult breathing. As though something was brewing inside you. You broke into a fit of coughing, barely able to stop. I raised you slightly, propping your back up against my chest. You breathed easier that way. You mumbled something or other. I wept, Gustav. I realized that I had to weep for all the music that would never come forth from you—and not because I would end up without you. I understood that, needless to say. I simply had the privilege of being here. At times for you, at others just to exist. Great talents require . . . nurturing. Whatever that may involve. I always felt a tremendous responsibility toward you, and toward your work.

I'm beginning to speak of you in the past tense. I'm getting used to it. A person adjusts. One day when I'm sitting alone in this train, I'll get used to that as well. Someone might proffer their hand. Someone might look at me. Perhaps I will look at someone. I don't know, Gustav. I don't know what will happen. I only know that these kinds of circumstances will stop occurring, but that doesn't mean that they will cease to exist. They will go on, and I will endure and withstand them every day in different ways. One day I'll be gone too. But these events will be remembered even then by someone. Memorable loves, devoted and worthy, are never forgotten. Neither are talents, nor follies.

Munich, September 12, 1910. An unparalleled gathering. Symphony No. 8, double orchestra and huge choir. What a spectacle! I was honestly scared. It was too much in every way. You paused, took a bow, and raised your baton in the air. Then, with a single stroke you sliced the air. I shivered. It was truly a communion among worlds, not of people. If, one day, someone were to venture out into the universe, that person need be a composer. No one else would be able to recreate the way in which the stars talk among themselves.

It was a magnificent spectacle. You were at your zenith. You were exhausted. It appeared as if you might collapse on stage. You smiled and stretched out your arms wide in the air, as if you wanted to embrace all those present. As if you wanted to embrace all of Munich. And I knew that you were embracing the universe. That's why I smiled too. I tore the orchid from my lapel and threw it onto the stage. Even in the loud applause I heard it fall. You picked it up and threw it back into the crowd, and in your outstretched hand I caught a glimpse of an immense truth: things must end. That's when I realized that you would never be happy. There is no music that goes on forever, just as there is no person who lives on forever. I knew that that was for the best. In your open hand there was a yearning for the unattainable. One of the saddest moments on stage, Gustav.

Don't stop, Alma. Memories are essential. You have to have something to live for now and tomorrow. Whatever is left.

"We will love each other forever," I whispered to you, and you began to cough heavily again.

Symphony No. 9

Rondo-Burleske: Allegro assai

THERE'S SOMETHING I MUST tell you, Gustav.

I fell in love with the idea of being Alma Mahler. Then I fell in love with you.

Assurances? No. What kind of assurances are you talking about? I could have had that from any number of men. Indeed, I did have it from quite a few. I reveled in your greatness, which I later came to learn largely meant profound sorrow. Immense loneliness. Great effort. Considerable. Numerous sacrifices. Umpteen missed birthdays, countless significant dates forgotten, unshared beds. Symphonies, concerts, different towns, changing residences, searching for new homes, suitcases, packing up our entire lives, undoing stability, living out of a suitcase, makeup, tears, silence, sadness, silence, tears, makeup, grief, suitcases, anguish. Sorrow!

The reason I fell in love with the idea of being with you was the lack of personal concerns in the life of one whose days passed by uneventfully; and though most of my days were unremarkable, I was able to live my life vicariously through you. I observed life all around me. You can't evade the things that surround you, you can't avoid seeing them. Around me was just yours, which was never ours, nor will it ever be. Despite your reserved manner, I take much of the responsibility for the making of Gustav Mahler. Because I am Alma Mahler. Not some unassuming woman, not an ordinary factory worker, a cook, a nanny, or what have you. I am and always have been Alma Mahler. And, so, don't ask me about assurances. What is certain is that, one day, all of this will stop being certain. A day that may be tomorrow. Do you think people are concerned with how miracles come about? Don't give it another thought. What's important for them is to possess them. To witness them. To experience them. To believe in them. Every miracle requires an act of faith, Gustav. And I never stopped believing in you. At one time, perhaps, I stopped believing in Gustav the husband or Gustav the father, but never in Gustav Mahler. The universe exists for miracles to abound within it. Within you there was never anything else besides great marvels, comparable to resurrections. Such wonders. And I witnessed them with astonishment. They gave me strength. That's why I've remained and why I exist. They restored something within me. They brought me to life when I thought I was dead. They were equally as indispensable to me as they were miraculous. Within me you experienced the best and the worst simultaneously. That's how I learned to withstand all the existing ordeals, as well as the impending ones. Miracles, Gustav. Along with faith in those miracles. From this perspective there was never anything else.

There is no submission here. Just admiration. Reverence. Bowing down before greatness. There is acceptance. And the incarnation of greatness. Life has brought me all kinds of moments with you. All kinds of people. I have traveled much. I have been filled with pride. I became well-known. I became part of a living legend. Not everyone is afforded that kind of distinction. I know it was due to you. But I allowed myself to be a part of it. I could have gone away. One doesn't live for a man met by chance in a beautiful city where one spends a nice day. One lives in order to have beautiful days. And I had none. None. I was in need of them. I had a table set for dinner at which you never came, writing implements that I never used, children who either ceased being that or who were just absent. Do you know what I have left from all that today? I have a living being who will soon be dead and nothing more. That's what I have.

There's something I must tell you, Gustav.

I took a liking to Alma Mahler who was not Alma Schindler. I basked in her. Particularly in those first few years. After that I lost her, only to find her again from time to time. For her to return in all her glory. I was someone who desperately wanted to be a woman all along. I didn't have that with you. There were many things I didn't have with you, and those I did were pointless. That's when Max appeared. He stared at me with eyes you no longer had for me. He made me feel like a woman in all my glory. He told me how beautiful I was, how precious, how trapped I was with you. He told me that something had faded in me, but when he ran his lips down my neck, that faded part was brought to life. One must maintain one's love for oneself: that's why there's so much love in the word "lover."

You asked me to choose between you and Max. To choose between duty and love. You know I loved him. But, even today, what I feel toward you transcends the limits of love, and it becomes something else. It isn't obligation. Nor sacrifice. Even though love entails numerous responsibilities and sacrifices, in this relationship it becomes something as basic as the desire to have a bad day. One must give oneself permission to have bad days. I need a good day. I need many good days, Gustav. But only a few of them remain.

June 26, 1912. Vienna. Vienna that I experienced with open arms, in a way that I never experienced you. The final symphony. There's no time, Gustav. I could forget this moment and everything after it. Nobody will forgive your worst if they don't appreciate your best. Symphony No. 9. It seems like a swan song, doesn't it? It does. That's what it suggests. It will come to symbolize that in a time that is yet to come. A time we won't see. We will always have the time that we lived. As for the rest . . .

Is there anything left, Gustav?

Sketch for Symphony No. 10
The final appearance of the sun.

Andante – Adagio

A SIMPLE TRUTH, MY beloved.

Love remains after death. No love ever dies. There's just forgotten love, in which case it was never love in the first place. This train will take us back to the beginning. Time has made you what you are, so that I may be much more than what my natural predispositions would have allowed. That's why people come together, in order to thrive, more than they had expected. After this journey things won't be the same. They'll remain the way you made them, the way I accepted them. Things that were once something, and that now may become nothing. Nothing—that's what frightens me most of all. But one who was something cannot become nothing. That which is something is cherished over time, at least in memories. And that which is remembered most of all is music, because it always stays the same. Its form never changes. No dust settles on it. There are no reckless spectators who would break its bounds or sully its purity. Music retains its original form, and in that way matters. And radiates. It radiates all that's within it: memories, people, events, states of the soul, states of mind, assumed states, states that are seemingly forgotten, as well as desired states. One's impressions, I would say. All that one has acquired and nurtured. That cleansed one. What was most beloved. One's first love. No—one's only love. Any love that comes to pass spurs growth. It takes root. Like something within that grows larger, until one day it bursts from the enormity of its size. When it bursts, it scatters all around and spreads. That's how love expands. That's how music proliferates. But not how I expand my chest when I draw in breath. I've learned to take in small breaths. And yet, I needed as much air as the universe contains. Love often hinders breathing, you know. And one often feels there's no air anywhere. No place where one might catch one's breath. Then a happy moment comes along and the fight for breath is justified. Then, for a moment, one's chest expands.

You left me with a scar, Gustav. A wound. One that will never heal. Into which I will hurl you, and into which your absence will fling you. Every day. You can't enter into another life if you don't bring with you all your previous loves. That's how much you hurt me, Gustav. As much as all the loves that have ever been and ever will be.

Gustav! I don't have time, Gustav! I don't! That's how much you hurt me! You left me precious little time! You squandered mine. Used it all up. I wasted my time on a living corpse. A noble cause? Kindness? No, no, Gustav! A desire for happiness. At the same time, both an outmoded desire and a missed chance for happiness.

You can manage alone, Alma. You can make do. You'll find another lone wolf in the world. There's still a lot left to happen. It doesn't have to end here. It needn't end.

Scherzo

LISTEN CAREFULLY TO ME now, I don't have much time.

Why did you do it? Why did you neglect me, Gustav? Why did you allow me to displace you? Love must never be supplanted. It mustn't ever. When it begins to tear apart, you have to sew it back together. Tell your beloved that her place is at home. To be there. Keep it warm. Create a meaningful place out of it. I had such vile, meaningless days! Monstrous! Damn you, Gustav! Curse you! You drained me like a water supply and left me dry, without means to replenish myself. And I have only one life, you know. One! With precious little left of it now. At all. Do you realize how much we could have had if only you were prepared to work on the small and happy moments? To allow them to happen? Very little is required for happiness. Miracles aren't necessary. What's required is simply the recognition that, at a given moment, there exists one and only one person for whom one's heart sings. Who means everything to you. That's all that's required.

I need . . . I need nothing, Gustav. I want nothing. I'm to blame for everything that's never happened. Not you. You can't force a person to love you the way he worships his greatest passion. You can simply either be a part of that love or not. I wanted much, but always I was satisfied with little.

Curse you, Gustav.

Be damned.

And I with you.

Purgatorio. Allegro moderato.

AND WHY ALL THESE tears? They don't make things any easier for me. Nor will they ever.

"Alma?" you whispered.

Again, I gently took your face in my hands.

"Does all of this have any meaning now?"

You looked into my eyes. I took off your glasses. I kissed your closed eyelids.

"There'll never be anything greater," I said to you, caressing your face.

We said our goodbyes to one another, Gustav.

I took care of you. I never stopped caring for you. I never will. A solemn pledge, Gustav. Most earnest.

Scherzo

"ALMA?" a whisper.

"Gustav?" tears.

"You were everything to me, Alma. Music was second. And there are so many unhearing ears."

Tears.

You smiled.

"Love, Alma. Nothing else remains."

"There was never anything else, Gustav."

Tears. A drawn-out breath.

"I love you," I whispered through tears.

"I love you, Alma," a whisper with closed eyes.

Vienna. May 18, 1911. Bells. I wasn't crying. Love doesn't forgive tears. I raised my head. I kissed your lips. You appeared so calm. For the first time you were still. A whole hour went by. Then the doctor arrived. Compassion. A terribly hot day. An uncomfortably tight black dress. A big black hat. Black gloves. A black mourning veil. The widow Mahler. Many people. Sketch for Symphony No. 10. I didn't cry. Perhaps because I had no tears in me. Perhaps because I knew that I mustn't cry. For a while I thought of other things: our suitcases, other people. A hellishly hot day. After that I came home. Symphony No. 10. I took off my dress. I stood upright in front of a mirror.

Alma Mahler. With bluish lips. Hands that are shaking. Pale skin. Madness in her eyes. Dark hair. Somber life. I fell upon my knees and cried out. I screamed. The dead of night. You will never write such music.

Finale

Alma Mahler.

Timeworn suitcases crammed with truth.
Timeworn suitcases crammed with pain.
Declining years.
Missed moments of happiness.
Numerous misfortunes.
Wounds to the soul.
Triumphs.
Gustav Mahler.
Luminary.
Greatness.
Music.
That's all that will remain.
Music.

There's no greater curse than an invisible curse. There's no greater love than that which demands nothing in return. That is how I am. Close your eyes. Dream. I will safeguard your dream the same way that I safeguarded your life. That is who I am. I will take care of you, Gustav. I will look after you. As if it were someone saving me from oblivion.

Stories exist to be told, and storytelling is nothing but a rewriting of the past in the eternal present.

Musical notation is an expression of eternal love. A final story without end. The notes separate the sound from the tone and the tone creates a specific feeling—a specific feeling in a particular story.

This story begins right here: in the separation between the tones and the sounds, in the transition from living life to living love. And all for just a brief moment.

That's how it's told. And that's how it leaves an impression. In an instant.

Alma Mahler is nothing but an endless repetition of music whose origin is love that, in and of itself, is sufficient basis for living.

Love in an instant that lasts an eternity.

— Sasho Dimoski
May 2014

SASHO DIMOSKI was born in Ohrid, Macedonia in 1985. He studied comparative literature at the Faculty of Philology Blaze Koneski in Skopje. He is the author of three novels as well as a collection of dramatic texts. He currently works as a dramatist at Teatar Dzinot in Veles, Macedonia.

PAUL FILEV is a freelance translator and editor. His translations from the Macedonian include *The Last Summer in the Old Bazaar* by Vera Buzarovska and *Alma Mahler* by Sasho Dimoski. He lives in Melbourne, Australia.

MICHAL AJVAZ, *The Golden Age.*
The Other City.

PIERRE ALBERT-BIROT, *Grabinoulor.*

YUZ ALESHKOVSKY, *Kangaroo.*

SVETLANA ALEXIEVICH, *Voices from Chernobyl.*

FELIPE ALFAU, *Chromos.*
Locos.

JOAO ALMINO, *Enigmas of Spring.*

IVAN ÂNGELO, *The Celebration.*
The Tower of Glass.

ANTÓNIO LOBO ANTUNES, *Knowledge of Hell.*
The Splendor of Portugal.

ALAIN ARIAS-MISSON, *Theatre of Incest.*

JOHN ASHBERY & JAMES SCHUYLER, *A Nest of Ninnies.*

GABRIELA AVIGUR-ROTEM, *Heatwave and Crazy Birds.*

DJUNA BARNES, *Ladies Almanack.*
Ryder.

JOHN BARTH, *Letters.*
Sabbatical.
Collected Stories.

DONALD BARTHELME, *The King.*
Paradise.

SVETISLAV BASARA, *Chinese Letter.*
Fata Morgana.
In Search of the Grail.

MIQUEL BAUÇÀ, *The Siege in the Room.*

RENÉ BELLETTO, *Dying.*

MAREK BIENCZYK, *Transparency.*

ANDREI BITOV, *Pushkin House.*

ANDREJ BLATNIK, *You Do Understand.*
Law of Desire.

LOUIS PAUL BOON, *Chapel Road.*
My Little War.
Summer in Termuren.

ROGER BOYLAN, *Killoyle.*

IGNÁCIO DE LOYOLA BRANDÃO, *Anonymous Celebrity.*
Zero.

BRIGID BROPHY, *In Transit.*
The Prancing Novelist.

GABRIELLE BURTON, *Heartbreak Hotel.*

MICHEL BUTOR, *Degrees.*
Mobile.

G. CABRERA INFANTE, *Infante's Inferno.*
Three Trapped Tigers.

JULIETA CAMPOS, *The Fear of Losing Eurydice.*

ANNE CARSON, *Eros the Bittersweet.*

ORLY CASTEL-BLOOM, *Dolly City.*

LOUIS-FERDINAND CÉLINE, *North.*
Conversations with Professor Y.
London Bridge.

HUGO CHARTERIS, *The Tide Is Right.*

ERIC CHEVILLARD, *Demolishing Nisard.*
The Author and Me.

MARC CHOLODENKO, *Mordechai Schamz.*

EMILY HOLMES COLEMAN, *The Shutter of Snow.*

ERIC CHEVILLARD, *The Author and Me.*

LUIS CHITARRONI, *The No Variations.*

CH'OE YUN, *Mannequin.*

ROBERT COOVER, *A Night at the Movies.*

STANLEY CRAWFORD, *Log of the S.S.*
The Mrs Unguentine.
Some Instructions to My Wife.

RALPH CUSACK, *Cadenza.*

NICHOLAS DELBANCO, *Sherbrookes.*
The Count of Concord.

NIGEL DENNIS, *Cards of Identity.*

PETER DIMOCK, *A Short Rhetoric for Leaving the Family.*

ARIEL DORFMAN, *Konfidenz.*

COLEMAN DOWELL, *Island People.*
Too Much Flesh and Jabez.

RIKKI DUCORNET, *Phosphor in Dreamland.*
The Complete Butcher's Tales.

RIKKI DUCORNET (cont.), *The Jade Cabinet.*
The Fountains of Neptune.

WILLIAM EASTLAKE, *Castle Keep.*
Lyric of the Circle Heart.

JEAN ECHENOZ, *Chopin's Move.*

STANLEY ELKIN, *A Bad Man*.
The Dick Gibson Show.
The Franchiser.

FRANÇOIS EMMANUEL, *Invitation to a Voyage*.

SALVADOR ESPRIU, *Ariadne in the Grotesque Labyrinth*.

LESLIE A. FIEDLER, *Love and Death in the American Novel*.

JUAN FILLOY, *Op Oloop*.

GUSTAVE FLAUBERT, *Bouvard and Pécuchet*.

JON FOSSE, *Aliss at the Fire*.
Melancholy.
Trilogy.

FORD MADOX FORD, *The March of Literature*.

MAX FRISCH, *I'm Not Stiller*.
Man in the Holocene.

CARLOS FUENTES, *Christopher Unborn*.
Distant Relations.
Terra Nostra.
Where the Air Is Clear.
Nietzsche on His Balcony.

WILLIAM GADDIS, JR., *The Recognitions*.
JR.

JANICE GALLOWAY, *Foreign Parts*.
The Trick Is to Keep Breathing.

WILLIAM H. GASS, *Life Sentences*.
The Tunnel.
The World Within the Word.
Willie Masters' Lonesome Wife.

GÉRARD GAVARRY, *Hoppla! 1 2 3*.

ETIENNE GILSON, *The Arts of the Beautiful*.
Forms and Substances in the Arts.

C. S. GISCOMBE, *Giscome Road*.
Here.

DOUGLAS GLOVER, *Bad News of the Heart*.

WITOLD GOMBROWICZ, *A Kind of Testament*.

PAULO EMÍLIO SALES GOMES, *P's Three Women*.

GEORGI GOSPODINOV, *Natural Novel*.

JUAN GOYTISOLO, *Juan the Landless*.
Makbara.
Marks of Identity.

JACK GREEN, *Fire the Bastards!*

JIŘÍ GRUŠA, *The Questionnaire*.

MELA HARTWIG, *Am I a Redundant Human Being?*

JOHN HAWKES, *The Passion Artist*.
Whistlejacket.

ELIZABETH HEIGHWAY, ED., *Contemporary Georgian Fiction*.

AIDAN HIGGINS, *Balcony of Europe*.
Blind Man's Bluff.
Bornholm Night-Ferry.
Langrishe, Go Down.
Scenes from a Receding Past.

ALDOUS HUXLEY, *Antic Hay*.
Point Counter Point.
Those Barren Leaves.
Time Must Have a Stop.

JANG JUNG-IL, *When Adam Opens His Eyes*

DRAGO JANČAR, *The Tree with No Name*.
I Saw Her That Night.
Galley Slave.

MIKHEIL JAVAKHISHVILI, *Kvachi*.

GERT JONKE, *The Distant Sound*.
Homage to Czerny.
The System of Vienna.

JACQUES JOUET, *Mountain R*.
Savage.
Upstaged.

JUNG YOUNG-MOON, *A Contrived World*.

MIEKO KANAI, *The Word Book*.

YORAM KANIUK, *Life on Sandpaper*.

ZURAB KARUMIDZE, *Dagny*.

PABLO KATCHADJIAN, *What to Do*.

JOHN KELLY, *From Out of the City*.

HUGH KENNER, *Flaubert, Joyce and Beckett: The Stoic Comedians*.
Joyce's Voices.

DANILO KIŠ, *The Attic*.
The Lute and the Scars.
Psalm 44.
A Tomb for Boris Davidovich.

ANITA KONKKA, *A Fool's Paradise*.

GEORGE KONRÁD, *The City Builder.*

TADEUSZ KONWICKI, *A Minor Apocalypse.*
The Polish Complex.

ELAINE KRAF, *The Princess of 72nd Street.*

JIM KRUSOE, *Iceland.*

AYSE KULIN, *Farewell: A Mansion in Occupied Istanbul.*

EMILIO LASCANO TEGUI, *On Elegance While Sleeping.*

ERIC LAURRENT, *Do Not Touch.*

VIOLETTE LEDUC, *La Bâtarde.*

LEE KI-HO, *At Least We Can Apologize.*

EDOUARD LEVÉ, *Autoportrait.*
Suicide.

MARIO LEVI, *Istanbul Was a Fairy Tale.*

DEBORAH LEVY, *Billy and Girl.*

JOSÉ LEZAMA LIMA, *Paradiso.*

OSMAN LINS, *Avalovara.*
The Queen of the Prisons of Greece.

ALF MACLOCHLAINN, *Out of Focus.*
Past Habitual.

RON LOEWINSOHN, *Magnetic Field(s).*

YURI LOTMAN, *Non-Memoirs.*

D. KEITH MANO, *Take Five.*

MINA LOY, *Stories and Essays of Mina Loy.*

MICHELINE AHARONIAN MARCOM, *The Mirror in the Well.*

BEN MARCUS, *The Age of Wire and String.*

WALLACE MARKFIELD, *Teitlebaum's Window.*
To an Early Grave.

DAVID MARKSON, *Reader's Block.*
Wittgenstein's Mistress.

CAROLE MASO, *AVA.*

HISAKI MATSUURA, *Triangle.*

LADISLAV MATEJKA & KRYSTYNA POMORSKA, EDS., *Readings in Russian Poetics: Formalist & Structuralist Views.*

HARRY MATHEWS, *Cigarettes.*
The Conversions.
The Human Country.
The Journalist.
My Life in CIA.

Singular Pleasures.
The Sinking of the Odradek.
Stadium.
Tlooth.

JOSEPH MCELROY, *Night Soul and Other Stories.*

ABDELWAHAB MEDDEB, *Talismano.*

GERHARD MEIER, *Isle of the Dead.*

HERMAN MELVILLE, *The Confidence-Man.*

AMANDA MICHALOPOULOU, *I'd Like.*

STEVEN MILLHAUSER, *The Barnum Museum.*
In the Penny Arcade.

RALPH J. MILLS, JR., *Essays on Poetry.*

CHRISTINE MONTALBETTI, *The Origin of Man.*
Western.

NICHOLAS MOSLEY, *Accident.*
Assassins.
Catastrophe Practice.
Hopeful Monsters.
Imago Bird.
Natalie Natalia.
Serpent.

WARREN MOTTE, *Fiction Now: The French Novel in the 21st Century.*
Oulipo: A Primer of Potential Literature.

GERALD MURNANE, *Barley Patch.*
Inland.

YVES NAVARRE, *Our Share of Time.*
Sweet Tooth.

DOROTHY NELSON, *In Night's City.*
Tar and Feathers.

WILFRIDO D. NOLLEDO, *But for the Lovers.*

BORIS A. NOVAK, *The Master of Insomnia.*

FLANN O'BRIEN, *At Swim-Two-Birds.*
The Best of Myles.
The Dalkey Archive.
The Hard Life.
The Poor Mouth.
The Third Policeman.

CLAUDE OLLIER, *The Mise-en-Scène.*
Wert and the Life Without End.

PATRIK OUŘEDNÍK, *Europeana*.
The Opportune Moment, 1855.

BORIS PAHOR, *Necropolis*.

FERNANDO DEL PASO, *News from
the Empire*.
Palinuro of Mexico.

ROBERT PINGET, *The Inquisitory*.
Mahu or The Material.
Trio.

MANUEL PUIG, *Betrayed by Rita Hayworth*.
The Buenos Aires Affair.
Heartbreak Tango.

RAYMOND QUENEAU, *The Last Days*.
Odile.
Pierrot Mon Ami.
Saint Glinglin.

ANN QUIN, *Berg*.
Passages.
Three.
Tripticks.

ISHMAEL REED, *The Free-Lance
Pallbearers*.
The Last Days of Louisiana Red.
Ishmael Reed: The Plays.
Juice!
The Terrible Threes.
The Terrible Twos.
Yellow Back Radio Broke-Down.

RAINER MARIA RILKE,
The Notebooks of Malte Laurids Brigge.

JULIÁN RÍOS, *The House of Ulysses*.
Larva: A Midsummer Night's Babel.
Poundemonium.

ALAIN ROBBE-GRILLET, *Project for a
Revolution in New York*.
A Sentimental Novel.

AUGUSTO ROA BASTOS, *I the Supreme*.

DANIËL ROBBERECHTS, *Arriving in
Avignon*.

JEAN ROLIN, *The Explosion of the
Radiator Hose*.

OLIVIER ROLIN, *Hotel Crystal*.

ALIX CLEO ROUBAUD, *Alix's Journal*.

JACQUES ROUBAUD, *The Form of
a City Changes Faster, Alas, Than the
Human Heart*.

The Great Fire of London.
Hortense in Exile.
Hortense Is Abducted.
*Mathematics: The Plurality of Worlds of
Lewis*.
Some Thing Black.

RAYMOND ROUSSEL, *Impressions of
Africa*.

VEDRANA RUDAN, *Night*.

GERMAN SADULAEV, *The Maya Pill*.

TOMAŽ ŠALAMUN, *Soy Realidad*.

LYDIE SALVAYRE, *The Company of Ghosts*.

LUIS RAFAEL SÁNCHEZ, *Macho
Camacho's Beat*.

SEVERO SARDUY, *Cobra & Maitreya*.

NATHALIE SARRAUTE, *Do You Hear
Them?*
Martereau.
The Planetarium.

STIG SÆTERBAKKEN, *Siamese*.
Self-Control.
Through the Night.

ARNO SCHMIDT, *Collected Novellas*.
Collected Stories.
Nobodaddy's Children.
Two Novels.

ASAF SCHURR, *Motti*.

GAIL SCOTT, *My Paris*.

JUNE AKERS SEESE,
Is This What Other Women Feel Too?

BERNARD SHARE, *Inish*.
Transit.

VIKTOR SHKLOVSKY, *Bowstring*.
Literature and Cinematography.
Theory of Prose.
Third Factory.
Zoo, or Letters Not about Love.

PIERRE SINIAC, *The Collaborators*.

KJERSTI A. SKOMSVOLD,
The Faster I Walk, the Smaller I Am.

JOSEF ŠKVORECKÝ, *The Engineer of
Human Souls*.

GILBERT SORRENTINO, *Aberration of
Starlight*.
Blue Pastoral.
Crystal Vision.

Imaginative Qualities of Actual Things.
Mulligan Stew.
Red the Fiend.
Steelwork.
Under the Shadow.
ANDRZEJ STASIUK, *Dukla.*
Fado.
GERTRUDE STEIN, *The Making of Americans.*
A Novel of Thank You.
PIOTR SZEWC, *Annihilation.*
GONÇALO M. TAVARES, *A Man: Klaus Klump.*
Jerusalem.
Learning to Pray in the Age of Technique.
LUCIAN DAN TEODOROVICI, *Our Circus Presents...*
NIKANOR TERATOLOGEN, *Assisted Living.*
STEFAN THEMERSON, *Hobson's Island.*
The Mystery of the Sardine.
Tom Harris.
JOHN TOOMEY, *Sleepwalker.*
Huddleston Road.
Slipping.
DUMITRU TSEPENEAG, *Hotel Europa.*
The Necessary Marriage.
Pigeon Post.
Vain Art of the Fugue.
La Belle Roumaine.
Waiting: Stories.
ESTHER TUSQUETS, *Stranded.*
DUBRAVKA UGRESIC, *Lend Me Your Character.*
Thank You for Not Reading.
TOR ULVEN, *Replacement.*
MATI UNT, *Brecht at Night.*
Diary of a Blood Donor.
Things in the Night.
ÁLVARO URIBE & OLIVIA SEARS, EDS., *Best of Contemporary Mexican Fiction.*
ELOY URROZ, *Friction.*
The Obstacles.
LUISA VALENZUELA, *Dark Desires and the Others.*
He Who Searches.

PAUL VERHAEGHEN, *Omega Minor.*
BORIS VIAN, *Heartsnatcher.*
TOOMAS VINT, *An Unending Landscape.*
ORNELA VORPSI, *The Country Where No One Ever Dies.*
AUSTRYN WAINHOUSE, *Hedyphagetica.*
MARKUS WERNER, *Cold Shoulder.*
Zundel's Exit.
CURTIS WHITE, *The Idea of Home.*
Memories of My Father Watching TV.
Requiem.
DIANE WILLIAMS, *Excitability: Selected Stories.*
DOUGLAS WOOLF, *Wall to Wall.*
Ya! & John-Juan.
JAY WRIGHT, *Polynomials and Pollen.*
The Presentable Art of Reading Absence.
PHILIP WYLIE, *Generation of Vipers.*
MARGUERITE YOUNG, *Angel in the Forest.*
Miss MacIntosh, My Darling.
REYOUNG, *Unbabbling.*
ZORAN ŽIVKOVIĆ , *Hidden Camera.*
LOUIS ZUKOFSKY, *Collected Fiction.*
VITOMIL ZUPAN, *Minuet for Guitar.*
SCOTT ZWIREN, *God Head.*

AND MORE...